STRANGER TRUTHS

# STRANGER TRUTHS

Maureen Passmore

*The Kent State University Press*

*Kent & London*

© 2005 by Maureen Passmore
All rights reserved
Library of Congress Catalog Card Number 2004025485
ISBN 0-87338-833-X
Manufactured in the United States of America

09  08  07  06  05      5  4  3  2  1

The Wick Poetry Chapbook Series is sponsored by the Stan and Tom Wick
Poetry Center and the Department of English at Kent State University.

Library of Congress Cataloging-in-Publication Data
Passmore, Maureen, 1973–
    Stranger truths / Maureen Passmore.
       p.   cm.—(Wick poetry chapbook series ; ser. 3, no. 10)
    ISBN 0-87338-833-X (pbk. : alk. paper) ∞
    I. Title.   II. Series.

PS3616.A863 S77 2005
811'.6—dc22                                              2004025485
British Library Cataloging-in-Publication data are available.

for David Teufel

# CONTENTS

## ACKNOWLEDGMENTS

Many thanks to Maggie Anderson for choosing this chapbook and for her great advice, and to Alice Cone, Kathy Method, and Sandra Clark for their kindness and help. Thank you to Sean M. Conrey and Frederick Barthelme, editors of the following publications in which some of these poems first appeared: *Sycamore Review* 16, no. 1, "Gulag Fun Park" and "The Fruit Woman"; and *Mississippi Review* 32, nos. 1–2, "Baltic Sun." Thanks to Dr. Michael M. Naydan for his expert advice on the Ukrainian language. Also, I am indebted to Sergei Zaitsev for first introducing me to Ukraine and to Wendell Mayo for suggesting I go to Lithuania. I appreciate Sharona Muir's urging to write about Ukraine. Many thanks to Larissa Szporluk for her endless encouragement, advice, and attention to these poems; she cared as much about their completion and success as I did. To my friends who lived in Ukraine with me—Bess, Anka, Roman, Petro, Dida, Gotsa, and Yvonne—next time I'll write about how much I loved it.

Most of all, thank you to my family and friends for their love, support, and for always sharing in my excitement, especially my parents, Alice and David Passmore, who always thought my love of language was a good thing.

All my love and appreciation to Dave, my enthusiastic supporter, first reader, and the one who encourages me to submit my poems in the first place.

## NOTE ON THE TEXT

I have used the transliterations of Ukrainian words rather than their more familiar Soviet-era counterparts, such as "Kyiv" instead of the Russian name of "Kiev," "Chornobyl" instead of "Chernobyl," and "Dnipro" for "Dnieper." Other Ukrainian words are italicized.

# KYIV CHECKPOINT

I still remember the hot metal and exhaust,
the *militsi* shouting, with pistols pointed high,
for all Americans to leave the bus. We five
walked out past frozen passengers, lost
to us. Men in fatigues demanded passports; one paused
at me and said, "You've a freckle in your eye,"
but I didn't understand the word "freckle."
I scrambled for my bag, and he laughed
at my quick movements. Another yelled,
"Documents or dollars," and it's almost funny,
but I'd never been so close to guns or men
whose mood controlled each second. The bus smelled
sour; we all stood unspeaking, not knowing what
to hand over, what would make their laughter end.

# RADIATION IN KYIV

Even when cautioned by the radio
to avoid the midday sun, the market women
sweat in it, standing next to umbrellas
that shade their huddled cabbages
and cherries. I pause to worry over
the black mole on an apple.

I think of Chornobyl women, who slept
that night with the windows open,
who sent their children to school,
ankle-deep in radioactive foam
to practice May Day songs.

The radio fuzzed for three days
with no warnings, until the women
packed into lead-windowed buses.
Their silverware would glow alone
for centuries. They return to husbands'
graves only once a year
because buried bones' half-lives can kill.

I stand, blocking other women's carts,
my cheeks already sunburned.
I know nothing of isotopes;
though I know that three reactors
still fire and cool
near the same apple orchards.

# BLESSING

Instead of just dead,
you are a *rusalka,*
a breasty water-spirit,
singing from birch branches
with a voice no man ignores.

You are waterborne,
dancing the *khorovod*
around lakes, in marshes,
in the grass. Your simple currency,
braided hair long as you are pure,
now spreads green and free,

down your back like a gown,
always wet.
No man will know your body
uncovered by weeds, no husband
will hear you sing to fir trees,

willing them your quick eyes,
gently rounded hips.
Instead you sing easily,
for no one is more beautiful
or free than *rusalki.*

In your lonely death,
blessed only by your mother
after the priest refused,
women send you their desires,
men never destroy you,
they just die in your hands.

## THE FRUIT WOMAN

I begin to love the fruit
woman in the market
when she offers *ozhina,*
blackberries bursting
with globed oceans, treats she knows
I can pay for, but I return
daily for the possibility
of hearing *oranzhevi*
whisper around her teeth
as she plumps a bag full
of oranges. She doesn't know
I drink only *chorni chai* for meals
instead of noodles-in-milk
in cracked cafeteria bowls
from the frowning attendant,
whose eyes flick down
to my shorts and bare legs,
who blesses my meal
with a *Smachnoho*
as if it's one more
word for "American."
After two days of "nothing to eat—
*nema*—" at the school,
the fruit woman nibbles
on the word *zakooziti,*
to share her secret
of what she's saved for me,
*hrooshi,* a handful of apricots
tiny and light as newborn mice.
The sound of her words,
gifts silking between her lips,
makes a small meal of fruit
a ripe mouth of song.

## GULAG FUN PARK

On a path in these woods, Lenin stands
thumbless, pointing toward Moscow. In one corner,
he's dressed for winter, long coat and scarf,
head lying sideways at his feet. Ina, I see
you at every tree, ticking your fingertips against
your palm, as if counting out the days
since your mother never returned.

Before a line of trees, Stalin is a bust
bigger than my body, the star on his uniform
bigger than my fanned fingers. Thick coins could fit
into the pupils of his granite eyes. Ina, only
two of him are left; they are armless.

You invite me for tea with broken cups,
used leaves, no sugar. You pace around
your chair, Ina, triple-tapping everything metal.
I tell you of yet another Stalin's chipped face,
the cheek left from a toppled monument,
how, when no one saw, I held it in my hands.

## BALTIC SUN

Almost midnight, I fall
half-asleep, watching hot air balloons
from the ninth floor. Here,
evening is when the sky
hesitates at dark blue,
sunlight a constant scrim
slung to the horizon.
If I squinted hard enough,
watched the glow cling down
and climb up the horizon, I'd see
his day roll around him,
miss nothing
of his fingers pulling at pens,
forks, keys, or skin.
But the light slows everything
in its ether: the birds stop yelling
to tuck their heads under
a wing, the insects slow their leg-rubbing.
The faraway fires of the balloons,
his breath in my ear,
are no longer hanging
in the slow burn of night.

# PANERIAI FOREST, LITHUANIA

Here, fingers inch underground,
searching through the soil, but not for us,
kettleheads with cameras. The bodies
don't wish to leave, to dig out.
Their veins grow and net the surrounding
earth. No one leaves a mass grave:
trees, absent sentries, line and clutch
them, careful mothers, and each of us
swallows the silence, watches the grass
clearing in the woods, straining to hear
them reach for one another,
for other bones to hold.

## LONYA TELLS ABOUT HIS YEARS
## IN THE KGB

I notice his gold wedding band
on a finger bending sideways
above the knuckle. I wonder
if he took off the ring during interrogation
beatings, or kept it on to remind himself
that, somewhere else, he was raising
two daughters. After the army, pushing
people off bridges into traffic was a good job.

*The first time, my boss placed a pistol*
*to my temple until I shoved; then, I smoked*
*a cigarette with each man first.*
*The girls had bows for their hair.*

Now, he buses Americans to each monument.
I could buy one of his military medals
and support his family for a year. Dollars
are supposed to bring democracy,
but they're more like smallpox,
a raging plague of full store shelves
met only with empty wallets.

*My wife came home, crying,*
*tell me, who can buy bread or milk now?*
*Everyone thought we had won a war.*

Lonya peels an orange with a knife,
hands me a ball of dripping pulp.
He could hate me, these fortunes I have
somehow, but doesn't.

Aldona left Lithuania on a road banked by trees. Her whole family walked on the road, keeping their eyes on the forest. Her mother sank to the ground in sudden labor. They held her head, women from other families, rubbed her legs, as if none of them were running, with jewelry belted in cloth under their clothes, from Soviet soldiers. Afterward, she washed her mother's legs with tea.

As we drive back to the city, slumped and lazy from gasoline fumes and clamped windows, we watch for children selling mushrooms on the side of the road. Aldona keeps a softly spoken tally of birds legging through the fields as we rumble past. We compare insects in new amber necklaces, watch for wooden wayside crosses, intricate totems erupting from the earth.

## KGB MUSEUM, VILNIUS

It's easier to talk about the greasy food and cold showers
than solitary confinement, its padded walls stained
with sweat and dirt rubbed from straightjackets.
Or the narrow, ground-floor openings to cells
where prisoners stood naked on ice blocks in winter.
Talk about the cool, rainy city instead of how hot
the execution chamber was, how we sidled
softly in slippers across its glass-encased floor but
still felt as if we were kicking up the dust of graves.
Decide how to explain that we paid to see misery,
to understand how fingernails are strong enough
to scratch names into concrete walls.

# BONE BLACK

Fingernails gone, bitten down,
except the one I save to scrape
my name, Arunas, into the wall.
My last canvas, I burned bones of birds,
rubbed them until a charcoal soil halved the cloth.
(Simona in bed with me, staring
from the lake of her black hair.)

The first night here, they shut me
in a closet, the sweatstains melting
off the walls, closing around
me. They asked my name,
the spelling of it, for hours.

Naked, standing on an ice block
in a winter cell—high window-slits.
The sky is white, Simona, a cold
I could never color. Bury the brushes
in the barn; I told them your name.

I move farther into the basement,
a new cell each month. They work
quickly. Once, I painted our horses
still tethered to the wagon, backs steaming,
the earth gouged brown behind them.
When they came for me, they knifed
the scene, chopped its frame into pieces.
Before sleep, my hands trace the water
of your hair on my pillow.

## TO FULFILL HER LIFE

Severing the braid from her daughter's head,
the mother covers the mirror over the bed,
smoothes the matron kerchief meant as a present,
and knots it at the girl's chin, only a blink hesitant.

*Grave, grouped men choose the boy and calm him with vodka.*

All forego the formal engagement, permission is understood,
the father carves her face below a knot in the wood.
The best friend tugs on the white dress, eyes barely looking.
Mother molds the *korovai,* women arrive for the cooking.

*The boy, alone, circles the village with bread and invitations.*

The priest washes the girl's brow, presses a cross into cold hands,
three times swings the incense to soften God's demands.
Mother and now aunts pinch the last doves out of the dough;
quiet and bereft, friends rush through gifts they're sewing.

*Uncles refuse entrance to the boy in gloomy tradition.*

Musicians clump at the village center; guests force their dance.
Holding wheat, they drink softly, sneak their glances,
shuffling behind the slow coffin cart. The couple is together
only during the walk, her fingers in his, a soft tether.

*Afterward, the boy ties the red scarf to the gate for her honor.*

A brother cradles the wedding wreath, a sister the flowers,
Mother moans the old songs, father blasts a gun to mark the hour.
In her white dress, her grave lined with proud linen,
the girl earns a place among the dead; her family rests, forgiven.

# TITANIUM STATUE ON THE DNIPRO RIVER

Dull sunlight sobers the sheen
on the Motherland monument's
breast, sword, and shield.
Veterans stop mourning at her feet
because she forever stands
at the moment they won the world.
Her chest puffs proud over the city,
eyes stern and cheeks chiseled into cliffs.

We speak on the ferry,
engine exhaust in our throats.
My friend speaks of battles
she won against a brother,
her mother indifferent as stone.
I'm thinking of my own hours
after school, sculpted against angry
hands, hardened against a brother
mute and brain-torn.

The boat shifts slowly on this gray river,
past the Mother who never corrodes,
no matter the elements.
From the bank she watches us,
curled leaves skimming the water.

## OLD TOWN, VILNIUS

I walked all around Old Town,
bending my feet over cobblestones,
searching for the last synagogue.
Past hundreds of churches,
white and wheat stucco,
vendors I asked closed their mouths,
shouldered away like prim cats.
A woman, mopping a church's marble
floor, crossed herself three times.

In a monastery garden,
narrow benches scattered with silent,
bearded men, palms open,
eyes shut against me.
A priest sold me a skinny candle
and a napkin to cover my head. I sank
down dark steps where dead monks lay
in cool tombs under the streets,
their hands old chicken bones
crossed over their chests.

Above, buildings bloated in corners,
bricks peeled apart as if to speak.
Seventeen men singing
in an unmarked facade are hard to find.
I stood and listened with the monks
from underneath the city.

## IF YOU LOVE HIM

Stop whistling when you walk with him.
Never give him a knife from your own

hand. Pass through his doorway without
touching, without kissing him: a house lives

in the space between you. Walk in socks
around the square of his room, show

that you mean no harm. Don't ask him
to close the windows or else you'll confuse

the drunken birds. The neighbor will ask if you're staying.
If she dies, she'll watch from the mirror

you failed to cover. You don't understand,
you are his weakness. Once a week, set out food

on the table, at a place where no one sits
unless you want someone he fears to possess it.

Know how to protect him from yourself. Bring
only eleven flowers or he'll think you're trying

to kill him. Remember to slice the bread
upside down, if you want this love.

Leave, place a coin on the table, but don't turn
back; just let him wave as you walk away.

# LEAVING UKRAINE

The tall, yellow-tipped grass
widened around us that last day
in the *Karpati*. We toed along
the train tracks with their constant
edge, arguing over which country
the mountains bordered, as if it mattered.

Dry leaves cracked under our feet,
any rain would've rolled off the earth
as if it were glass. We'd eaten
the last of the stale bread, shoved
in our pockets last night, to slow
the effects of a homebrew *horilka*,
made from potatoes withering
in their own rot. Petro asked
if I was ready to go home.

I couldn't finish a sentence
in English to say that small spears pierced
the birds living in my wrist bones.

We walked toward the trees
I could no longer name in the bowl
of my brain. I was starting to plow
under. The woman I was could die, knives
poking through her collarbones,
and this country would keep her,
bury her.

# FOURTH OF JULY, MISHA'S VILLAGE

On cramped sofas, we sit low to the table,
cans of his mother's homebrew crowding
the plates of meat, cucumbers, tomatoes.
The first three toasts honor Misha's
recent birthday; the rest of the evening,
Petro quietly finishes my glass
when no one's looking. I'm out
of water, want to go to sleep.
Misha's mother is singing, *Halyu moya,*
her eyes shut, cheeks shining.
Everyone stills, listening to her sing
to a daughter, *ya prishov po barvinok,*
buried outside the village.

Tomorrow, Anka wants to visit
the local graveyard. Driving here,
we passed an open-bed truck,
full of wreaths and loose flowers,
carrying a woman in an open box.
Her skin looked like baked meat
gathering flies in the sun.
Misha refills our glasses.

We eventually sneak
outside, wander down the road,
Misha's house the only light
for miles. We pass a dog growling
at a gate, and Misha turns back
up to his house. In the morning,
he'll show us the pond
where they used to swim. One more
week until we leave. I want to go
to sleep, to wake up in Kyiv,
on the morning we fly home.

# NOTES

1. BLESSING: The poetic image of a *rusalka* (or "water spirit") was inspired by its more factual representation in Dr. Linda Ivanits's *Russian Folk Belief* (Armonk, N.Y.: M. E. Sharpe, 1989).

2. THE FRUIT WOMAN: *Smachnoho* is the polite wish to have a good meal.

3. GULAG FUN PARK: Officially called the "Soviet Sculpture Garden at Grutas Park" in Druskininkai, Lithuania, this quiet place in the woods displays salvaged Soviet statues not crushed after independence.

4. PANERIAI FOREST, LITHUANIA: The site of a mass grave where Nazis murdered and buried Jews from Vilnius and the Lithuanian countryside.

5. TO FULFILL HER LIFE: This poem portrays different Slavic folk traditions. Young women who died before they were married were wedded to a young man at their funeral. Doing this ensured that the woman had gone through all the major stations of life before burial and, therefore, would not return to her village or family as a ghost.